Christmas Lights

Ann Fearrington

Houghton Mifflin Company
Boston 1996

For information about this and other Houghton Mifflin
trade and reference books and multimedia products, visit
The Bookstore at Houghton Mifflin on the World Wide Web
at http://www.hmco.com/trade/.

Manufactured in the United States of America

Book design by David Saylor
The text of this book is set in 24-point Giovanni Bold.
The illustrations are pastel and are reproduced in full color.

BVG   10   9   8   7   6   5   4   3   2   1

Library of Congress Cataloging-in-Publication Data
Fearrington, Ann.
Christmas lights / by Ann Fearrington.   p.   cm.
Summary: On Christmas night a family drives into town
to see the displays of Christmas lights.
ISBN 0-395-71036-7
[1. Christmas—Fiction. 2. Light—Fiction.] I. Title.
PZ7.F2966Ch 1996
[E]—dc20   94-25768   CIP   AC

To Vance, Mom and Dad, James, Joseph, Jonathan, Florence,
Jessica, Pass, Viola, and Caro, who have all sailed with me,
one Christmas or another, on the good ship "Four-Door".

—A. F.

On Christmas night
the air is cold and still.

A full moon
lights the narrow road.

Around the curve,

a dazzling spire!

How many lights?
Too many to count.

In the woods
a grandfather lights one tree
for each grandchild.

The road runs past the artist's house
with its stream of stars,

past the fast-food place
with its smiling snowman—

toward the lights of town.

By the pond,
twin trains shine.

Apartment balconies blaze.

Then a surprise:

the steam plant
puffs a wreath of smoke.

And an old favorite—

an office building like a box
for the biggest present in the world.

Winding streets are lined
with paper-bag lanterns.

There's a row of giant
peppermint sticks

and a house so bright
we can almost hear the lights:

blink, blink, dazzle, flash.
Gleam, glow, sparkle, shine!

On the way home,
one last burst of lights:
going, going, gone.

It's late now.

We're home.

Last year, this year,
every year,
we love our own lights
best of all.

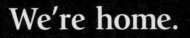

Good Christmas.
Good night.